"Too bad you can't go to Washington," Lucas said.

"It's okay," said Cricket, pretending that she didn't care. "I'll probably go with my own family one of these days."

"That's good," said Julio.

"Yeah," Lucas agreed. "Then you won't mind that Sara Jane Cushman is going with Zoe."

"What?" asked Cricket. "Are you making that up?"

SPRING BREAK

JOHANNA HURWITZ

SCHOLASTIC INC.

New York   Toronto   London   Auckland   Sydney
Mexico City   New Delhi   Hong Kong   Buenos Aires

ISBN 0-439-41977-8

Text copyright © 1997 by Joanna Hurwitz. All rights reserved. Published by Scholastic Inc., 557 Broadway, New York, NY 10012, by arrangement with HarperCollins Children's Books, a division of HarperCollins Publishers. SCHOLASTIC and associated logos are trademarks and/or registered trademarks of Scholastic Inc.

12 11 10 9 8 7 6 5 4 3   8 9/0

Printed in the U.S.A.   40

First Scholastic printing, March 2002

To my friend & pen pal
Leezie Borden

Contents

A Bad Break

One Wednesday in early April Cricket Kaufman was walking home from school. It was just two days before the spring vacation. Even though Cricket *loved* school, she was delighted that the week's holiday was almost here. She had so much to look forward to.

One of Cricket's fifth-grade classmates, Lucas Cott, was walking home too.

There were days when the two of them got along just fine. After all, even though there were four sections of each grade at the Edison-

Armstrong School, for some mysterious reason Lucas and Cricket had been in the same class every year.

There were some days, however, when Cricket wished she could say some magic word and just make Lucas Cott disappear. Today had been one of those days. He had belched, not once, not twice, but three times while she was in the midst of reading her book report aloud to the class. After the second belch Mr. Flores, their teacher, had scolded him. Lucas claimed it was because of the franks and beans he had eaten for lunch. Then he gave his third belch.

Cricket had serious doubts about whether it was the food inside Lucas that had caused him to act that way. Lucas had a reputation for pulling pranks and being a pain.

"Hey, Cricket," Lucas yelled. "Wait up."

"Why should I wait for you?" asked Cricket in disgust.

"All right. Don't walk with me. See if I care," said Lucas. "Is it true that you're going to Washington, D.C., with Zoe Mitchell during the vacation?" he called to her.

At this Cricket had to stop. "Yes," she said, beaming proudly. "It was all arranged last night.

Zoe's mother called my mother and invited me. Her father has to attend some sort of conference there, and Zoe and her mother and sister are all going along."

· Zoe had hinted to Cricket that perhaps she could accompany them on their trip. But when the invitation actually came the evening before, Cricket had nearly burst with excitement. She had never been to Washington. There was so much to see and visit there: the White House, the Washington Monument and the Lincoln Memorial, the Smithsonian Museum. They all were places she had heard about. The invitation was one of the most wonderful things that had ever happened to Cricket.

"So how come you're going too?" Lucas wanted to know.

"Zoe's parents decided that Zoe and Halley could each bring one friend. They're going to get two hotel rooms, and the kids will sleep in one and the grown-ups in the other. I've never stayed in a hotel before. Have you?" she asked Lucas.

"Yeah. Once when I was a baby. But I can't remember it at all, so it doesn't count." Lucas looked at Cricket. "You're really lucky," he said. "I'm not going anywhere or doing anything during the spring break."

Cricket shrugged. "You'll probably be busy goofing off with Julio and the other guys," she told him.

"Yeah. Maybe we'll go to a movie or something during the week. But I wish I could go away someplace special like you," he admitted. "Lucky duck."

"Well, when you think about people like Helen Keller, we're all lucky," Cricket pointed out. Helen Keller had been the subject of her book report. When Helen Keller was a little girl, she had gotten very sick and as a result had become blind and deaf. It had been very interesting to read about her. Everyone in their class had read a biography of someone famous. Lucas had read about a man named Jean-Henri Fabre, who had spent his whole life studying bugs. That was just like Lucas, to find something gross to read and write about.

"What did you get on your book report?" she asked him now.

"A," Lucas said.

Cricket wondered if Lucas was telling the truth. Of course *she* had gotten an A. She almost always did. And Mr. Flores had even written at the end of her report, *This is an excellent job. Congratulations.* She wondered if he had written anything on Lucas's paper.

The thought of the words on her book report

and the anticipation of the super trip ahead of her put Cricket in a wonderful mood. She really felt like the luckiest person alive.

Turning toward Lucas, she said, "Did you ever think what it would be like if you were blind?" While she was working on her report, she had sat in her bedroom with her eyes closed and tried to imagine it. Pretending that she was blind like Helen Keller, she had even gotten up from the chair by her desk. She had walked all the way to the door of her room without bumping into anything.

"Yeah," Lucas admitted. "And deaf too. Which do you think is worse?"

"Deaf," said Cricket without a moment's hesitation. She had given the matter serious thought while she was writing her report. "If you're deaf, you can't hear voices or music or anything."

"Yeah, but if you're blind, you can't even walk without falling over things—unless you have a Seeing Eye dog, of course," said Lucas.

"I bet I could walk all the way home without using my eyes and without a dog," Cricket asserted. "If you know the way, it's easy."

"I bet you can't," said Lucas.

"Can too," said Cricket.

"Can't," said Lucas. "I'll bet you." He stuck his

hand in his pocket and held out a nickel and three pennies and some lint. It wasn't very much. "I'll bet you my new wristwatch," he said, pulling up the sleeve of his jacket to show it off.

"You can't bet your watch," said Cricket.

"Why not? It's mine. And besides, you won't win it."

"Yes, I will," said Cricket firmly. "Watch me. Here I go."

Cricket closed her eyes and continued walking down the street. She smiled to herself as she moved. Lucas had been in such a hurry to make a bet with her that he had even forgotten to make her put up something in case she lost. She was certain that she would win the bet, but even if she had to open her eyes, she would not have to give Lucas anything but the temporary satisfaction that he was right. And it wouldn't even mean that he was right. Just that she hadn't managed to walk home with her eyes closed that day.

"Don't open your eyes," Lucas warned Cricket.

"They're shut, can't you see? Are you blind or something?" Cricket asked her classmate.

She continued walking slowly down the street. It was funny how she was aware of every step she took now that her eyes were closed.

"You better tell me when we reach the curb," Cricket said to Lucas.

"No way," said Lucas. "If you were blind, you wouldn't have me walking along the street with you. See. That's what I meant. You can't walk without looking."

Cricket didn't open her eyes. She knew that this conversation was a trick of Lucas's to make her lose the bet. So instead of giving up and watching where she was going, she slowed her pace even more. She felt the ground with her foot before she made each step. That way she'd be aware when she reached the curb. She also knew that no matter how mean or silly Lucas Cott could sometimes be, he'd never let her walk in front of a car. He wouldn't want her to get run over.

Cricket wiggled her shoulders and shifted her backpack. Walking so slowly made her aware of its weight. Helen Keller didn't have a backpack on when she walked down the street, she realized.

"Watch out," Lucas suddenly shouted.

But it was too late. Cricket tripped on a bump in the concrete sidewalk just at the edge of the curb. She landed in the street with a thud. There was a terrible pain in her right ankle, and her eyes were wide open.

"Are you okay?" asked Lucas, bending down. He really looked concerned, and he didn't even gloat that Cricket had lost the bet.

"I think so," whispered Cricket, trying hard not to cry. She attempted to get up, but her ankle buckled under her. The pain was the worst she had ever experienced. Tears started running down her cheeks. It hurt so much that she didn't even care if Lucas saw her crying. He'd have cried too if he'd had such a bad fall.

"Can you walk?" Lucas asked.

Cricket shook her head. "No," she whispered.

"Maybe you broke your leg," Lucas said in awe. "Do you think you could hop home?"

Cricket shook her head. The pain was so bad that it took her breath away. "No," she whispered again.

Lucas looked around. Sometimes going home from school, they passed mothers pushing baby carriages or other people out walking. But there was no one on the street this afternoon, just an occasional car driving by.

Lucas helped Cricket move out of the street and back onto the sidewalk. She sat helplessly looking at her right ankle.

"My mother has a friend who lives on the next

block," Lucas suddenly said. "Wait here, and I'll go to her house. She can drive you home."

Cricket watched Lucas run down the street. While he was gone, an older woman did walk by. She looked at Cricket crossly and said, "You can't sit here all day. You're blocking the way."

Cricket didn't have the energy to explain. She just nodded. From time to time she tried to move her ankle. She thought the pain might go away. But it seemed just as bad or maybe even worse each time she did that.

Finally a car pulled up. Lucas jumped out. "This is Mrs. Hooper," he called to Cricket. "You're lucky she was home. She was just getting ready to go out."

Mrs. Hooper and Lucas helped Cricket get into the backseat of the car. Within three minutes the car reached Cricket's house. And within ten minutes she was in her mother's car on her way to the hospital for X rays.

Cricket Kaufman had left school at three o'clock feeling like the luckiest girl in the world. By six o'clock her ankle was in a cast, and even though the pain was no longer so strong, she had gotten some very bad news.

"There's no way you can even think about

going to Washington," her mother told her.

By six o'clock, even with her perfect eyesight and good hearing, Cricket felt like the unluckiest girl in the world.

2
Stuck at Home

In the past, whenever Cricket had seen a kid walking with crutches, she had thought it must be great. First of all, kids on crutches got lots of extra attention. They sat in the front row at school activities and everyone was sympathetic toward them.

Furthermore, walking about on crutches *looked* like loads of fun. Wearing a plaster cast was pretty special too. Everyone wanted to sign casts. Cricket could remember the time back in second grade when she had written on the cast on Lizzy Gottlieb's arm. She had taken her green marker and printed *CRICKET* in bold letters. Lizzy had complained that she'd taken up too much space on the cast, but there was nothing she could do about it.

Now Cricket had a clean white cast to protect her ankle. The cast went halfway up her leg, and it wasn't any fun at all. It was heavy, and underneath the plaster it itched. But there was no way she could scratch her leg. Worst of all, she couldn't show the cast off.

"You can't go to school tomorrow," her mother said. "It's almost vacation time anyhow, so you won't miss any important work."

"But I want to go to school," Cricket said.

"First you must practice walking with the crutches," Mrs. Kaufman said.

"I hate the crutches," said Cricket. Who would have guessed that walking with crutches would be so difficult? It hurt under her arms when she walked with them, and she had to move so slowly. It was hard to sit down, and it was harder to get up.

"You'll get used to them," her father assured her.

"By the time you get really expert with the crutches, you won't need them anymore," said Mrs. Kaufman.

"Six to eight weeks!" Cricket complained.

That's how long the orthopedist had said Cricket would be wearing the cast.

The orthopedist's name was Dr. Schertle. "It rhymes with turtle," he had announced. He probably thought it was a joke and would make Cricket laugh. But she was too upset by his news about her ankle.

"I'm going to have to use these crutches for at least six weeks." Cricket counted on her fingers. By then it would be practically June. The whole spring would be lost. No Rollerblading, no jumping rope, no bike riding. Spring was the best season for all those activities. By the time she could do any of them again, it would be too hot.

"Think of all the things you *can* do," her mother pointed out. "You can practice the piano; you can read; you can do puzzles; you can write letters." Those were all activities that Cricket usually enjoyed. Somehow they sounded very boring now.

"But I can't go to Washington," said Cricket, and she began to cry. "I wanted to go so much," she said. "It was my lifelong dream to see the White House."

"You never, ever mentioned a word about Washington until Zoe's mother called," said her mother.

"A dream is something you've wanted for ages

and ages," Mr. Kaufman said.

"I didn't talk about it, but that doesn't mean that it wasn't my dream." Cricket sniffed. It was true she hadn't ever mentioned it specifically. Everyone in Cricket's class at school knew that she planned to become the first woman president of the United States. Then she would actually *live* in Washington, inside the White House. "Now I have to wait till I'm grown-up to see it."

"Of course you'll see the White House before you're an adult. It isn't going to run away. It's been there for a couple of hundred years. It can wait for you a little longer," said Cricket's father. "Our family can take a trip there in a few years, when Monica is a bit older."

Monica was Cricket's younger sister. She was two years old. Cricket knew that if they went to the White House with her now, Monica would run around the rooms and make so much noise that the president wouldn't be able to do any of his important work. Monica might even knock things off the tables. The White House wasn't baby-proofed the way the Kaufman house was.

"It's going to take forever for Monica to grow up," Cricket complained. "Besides, it's not the same. I wanted to go with Zoe."

Cricket had phoned Zoe on Wednesday evening when she returned from the medical center. She had to give her the bad news. Zoe had been properly sympathetic, as a good friend should be.

"It's so rotten!" Zoe had moaned into the telephone. "We would have had such a good time together. The hotel room has a tiny little refrigerator in it, and it's filled with candy bars and sodas. My dad had promised that we could each pick out one thing even though they charge an extra-high price for the things in the refrigerator. It would have been like a little party at night. And Halley's friend Lyndsey is really neat. You'd have liked her a lot. I do."

Cricket had sniffed into the telephone. "Will you send me a postcard?"

"I'll send you ten postcards!" said Zoe with passion. "And I'll buy you a souvenir too."

"Thanks," said Cricket, wiping her tears. "My parents said I can't go to school tomorrow. But if you come over here to visit me, you can be the first person to sign my cast."

"I can't come tomorrow," said Zoe. "Don't you remember that on Thursdays I have ballet lessons? And on Friday I have a dentist appointment. I probably won't be able to see you until we get back from Washington. But I'll call you every evening. I'll even call from Washington, if my parents will let me."

"Okay," said Cricket. "I won't let anyone sign my cast before you," she promised. That was the least she could do to make up to her best friend the loss of her company on the vacation trip.

That first night with the broken ankle was awful. Rather than make the effort of going upstairs to her bedroom, Cricket slept on the living room sofa. Her mother put a sheet on it and brought Cricket's pillow and blankets downstairs for her. Then, even though she had a painkiller to help her sleep, Cricket had a hard time. She couldn't find a comfortable position on the sofa. She had never thought about her legs before when she went to sleep. But now she realized that she usually curled up, and it was impossible to do that with a cast on one leg.

Thursday passed very slowly. Mrs. Kaufman helped Cricket take a sponge bath. They didn't use a sponge, just Cricket's old washcloth. But Mrs. Kaufman helped Cricket get washed without getting into the bathtub. The whole process made Cricket feel as if she were a baby, like Monica.

"I think in a few days we'll be able to work

something out so you can take a quick shower," her mother told Cricket. "I've heard that people wrap their casts in plastic to keep them from getting wet."

"What would happen if it got wet?" Cricket wanted to know.

"I suspect it dissolves," said Mrs. Kaufman.

Using her crutches, Cricket slowly moved from the bathroom into the kitchen. Since there wasn't any rush about getting off to school, there was time for her mother to make French toast for breakfast. That was good. Cricket banged her toes, which were sticking out of her cast, against the leg of the table. That was bad.

"I want sticks like Cricket," said Monica. She sat in her high chair eating breakfast.

"Cricket's sticks are called crutches," Mrs. Kaufman told her little daughter.

"I want crushes like Cricket," said Monica.

"Cricket needs her crutches to walk," said Mrs. Kaufman, wiping maple syrup off Monica's face.

After breakfast Mrs. Kaufman cleared the table. Then she brought Cricket her library book and her watercolor paints and her box of stationery. "Here are things that will keep you busy without moving," she told Cricket.

"What are you going to do?" Cricket asked her mother.

"Thursday's my grocery day," Mrs. Kaufman said. "It's less crowded than going tomorrow. So Monica and I are going shopping. Just ignore the phone if it rings. You don't have to attempt to answer it. The answering machine will record the message for me."

"Okay," Cricket said, sighing. In school they would just be doing their math work. Mr. Flores had a way of always making math interesting and fun. She wished she were sitting in her seat in class instead of in her kitchen at home. It was going to be a long, long day.

At the conclusion of the school day Cricket had a pair of visitors. After a long and dreary session of practicing her piano lesson, she was sitting in the living room when Lucas Cott and Julio Sanchez came to her house. Julio was president of the class, so he had a special reason for coming. "We all made get-well cards for you," he said, handing Cricket a large manila envelope.

"Thanks," said Cricket, taking the envelope from him. Over the years she had made get-well cards for loads of her classmates. This was the first time she had been on the receiving end.

"I can't believe I was walking with you when you fell yesterday," Lucas marveled. "Too bad you couldn't go to the hospital in an ambulance. It would have been fun to be inside and have the siren roaring as you went."

"No, it wouldn't," said Cricket. "Breaking an ankle is not fun. What happened in school today?" she asked her classmates.

"You know, the usual," said Lucas.

"Yeah," Julio agreed. "Math, social studies, reading, all the regular stuff." He thought for a moment. "The school lunch was extra good today," he added. "Sloppy joes and corn. Chocolate pudding for dessert." He licked his lips.

"I wouldn't have had it anyhow." Cricket sighed. "I always bring my lunch."

"That's true," Julio said.

"Can I try your crutches?" asked Lucas. He picked them up and put them under his arms before Cricket could give him an answer.

"Put them down. They're not toys," Cricket said.

"I will. I will. In a minute," said Lucas. Cricket noticed that he moved about the room with much more ease than she did. Maybe it was because he didn't actually need the crutches. She had to be careful not to bump her broken ankle as she moved.

"Can I sign your cast?" asked Julio. "I've never seen a cast that was so clean and white. Nobody's written on it yet."

"I'm waiting for Zoe. I promised her that she could be the first to sign it," said Cricket.

"We could sign on one side, and there would still be plenty of room for her name," said Lucas, putting down the crutches and admiring the cast.

"Is it cold with your toes sticking out like that?" Julio asked.

Cricket looked down at her bare toes on her right foot. "No," she said. "It's pretty warm inside the house."

"Too bad you can't go to Washington," Lucas said.

"It's okay," said Cricket, pretending that she didn't care. "I'll probably go with my own family one of these days."

"That's good," said Julio.

"Yeah," Lucas agreed. "Then you won't mind that Sara Jane Cushman is going with Zoe."

"What?" asked Cricket. "Are you making that up? April Fools' Day is over," she reminded Lucas.

"Hey," Lucas said. "I'm not making anything up. Didn't Zoe tell you? Her mother called up Sara

Jane's mother, and they invited Sara Jane to go to Washington with them. I heard them talking about it at lunchtime."

At that moment Cricket's mother and Monica entered the living room. "Lucas, Julio," Mrs. Kaufman greeted the two boys. "I've put out some milk and cookies in the kitchen. It was so sweet of you to come visit Cricket. I know it's made her feel good to see you both here. Come and have a snack now," she said to the boys.

"Cricket has crushes," Monica announced to Lucas and Julio.

"Yeah," Julio agreed.

Mrs. Kaufman handed Cricket the crutches so she could walk into the kitchen. But Cricket had no appetite for cookies. All she could think about was Zoe and Sara Jane Cushman. How could her best friend betray her that way?

Cricket was so angry at the thought of Sara Jane Cushman accompanying Zoe Mitchell to Washington that it hurt worse than breaking an ankle. She could not believe that Zoe could want to spend spring break with Sara Jane. Sara Jane was so boring. She never talked in class. She hardly even talked during lunchtime or recess. She had nothing to say. In fact, she was so quiet that usually you forgot that she was around. How could Zoe even think of inviting her to go to Washington?

Lucas and Julio finished the snack that Mrs. Kaufman had prepared for them. Monica ate two cookies. Lucas ate three cookies, and Julio four. Cricket only nibbled on one. Even her favorite chocolate cookies with peanut butter chips couldn't distract her from having angry thoughts toward Zoe.

"I hope you feel better," Julio said politely to Cricket as he got ready to leave.

"Yeah," Lucas agreed.

"Wait," Cricket called after them as the two boys headed to the door. "You can sign my cast right now if you want to." Why should she wait for Zoe Mitchell anyhow? Zoe wouldn't be coming to visit her until next week. By then Zoe and she might not even be best friends anymore. By then Zoe would probably be best friends with Sara Jane Cushman.

"Neat," said Julio.

He reached into his backpack and pulled out a ballpoint pen. He crouched down and wrote his name in big letters on Cricket's cast. Then he handed the pen to Lucas. Lucas wrote his first name, and he drew a smiley face on the cast too.

Cricket didn't feel the least bit smiley herself.

3

Mr. Flores Pays a Visit

That evening Zoe phoned Cricket. "Here," said Mr. Kaufman. "I'll help you get to the phone."

Cricket had just sat down in the big, comfortable living room chair. It had a matching footstool on which she could rest her leg. This was the chair that her father usually sat in. In the past she had always been pleased when she was able to sit in that chair and read. Now with her leg in a cast she again had that privilege, but she was too unhappy to enjoy it. She didn't feel like talking to Zoe either.

Mr. Kaufman held the crutches in one hand and gave Cricket the other to enable her to raise herself out of the chair. Slowly she made her way to the telephone. "We should have a cordless," she grumbled. "Zoe has one at her house. If we had one, I wouldn't have to get up."

Cricket's father smiled. "I didn't know you were going to break your ankle," he said.

"Hello," Cricket said glumly into the telephone.

"Cricket," Zoe replied. "I've got to tell you something."

"You don't have to tell me. I already know," said Cricket. "I can't believe it. And I think it's mean. How could you do that to me?"

"Well, it's not my fault that you broke your ankle," said Zoe, defending herself. "But my parents did say I could bring someone on the trip to Washington. And now you can't come. So since Halley is going to have a friend with her, I wanted to have someone come along too."

"Why did you pick Sara Jane Cushman?" asked Cricket angrily.

"I didn't know who else to ask," Zoe admitted. "Don't you remember that Kimberly's grandmother is coming to visit her? So she couldn't go away. And Jessica announced to the whole class that she's going to Disney World over spring break. She's been talking about it since she came back from Christmas vacation. You didn't expect me to invite Lucas Cott, did you?" asked Zoe.

In spite of herself, a small smile crossed Cricket's face. Of course Zoe and Halley and Halley's friend Lyndsey couldn't share a hotel room with Lucas Cott. And besides, Lucas would probably get into all sorts of trouble all over Washington.

"You're still my best friend. Honest," said Zoe.

"Cross your heart and hope to die?" asked Cricket, still not a hundred percent certain whether or not to forgive Zoe.

"Cross my heart. And remember, I'm going to send you lots of postcards and buy you a souvenir," Zoe told Cricket.

By the time Cricket got off the phone, she was feeling a little better. She remembered that Zoe's mother was in the same exercise class as Sara Jane's mother. Mrs. Mitchell knew the Cushmans' telephone number and just rushed to invite Sara Jane. Cricket couldn't blame Zoe for that.

On Friday afternoon, when the school day was over, Cricket had a surprise visitor. Mr. Flores came to see her. Cricket was amazed and flustered to see her teacher standing inside her living room. She had never heard of a teacher going to someone's home before.

"Cricket has crushes," Monica announced to the fifth-grade teacher as Cricket sat looking up at him wordlessly.

"Poor Cricket," said Mr. Flores. "Lucas told me all about your fall. He said you were walking with your eyes closed as if you were blind. Like Helen Keller."

Cricket turned bright red with embarrassment. Even though she had been fascinated by the life of Helen Keller when she read the book for her report, she didn't like being reminded about how her accident had occurred. It was just like Lucas to go around blabbing to the world how she had happened to fall.

"Anyhow, you'll be better before you know it," said Mr. Flores cheerfully. "I know you're a great reader, and that will help you pass the time. In fact, I stopped at the library and brought you some books that you might enjoy."

Cricket watched as her teacher opened his backpack and pulled out half a dozen library books.

"You don't have to make a report on any of these," he said, smiling at Cricket. He handed her one of the books. "This is a biography of Louis

Braille. He's the man who devised a technique so that blind people like Helen Keller were able to learn how to read. And here's a biography of Anne Sullivan Macy, who, as you know, was Helen's teacher."

Cricket licked her lips and wondered what to say. She knew it wasn't Helen Keller's fault that she had broken her ankle, but still, she wasn't as keen on her now as she had been before.

"These other books are all fiction," said Mr. Flores. "I hope there are at least a couple among them that you haven't already read. Your mother can return them when you've finished. You're so responsible I know I don't have to worry about that."

"Did you bring me homework to do too?" asked Cricket. These were the first words she had said since Mr. Flores had entered the room.

"No homework," said her teacher. "This is vacation time, remember? I'm going off on a hiking trip with my brother tomorrow. I won't be thinking about school for the next week, and I don't want you to think about it either. When the spring break is over, your parents and I will work out a way for you to get to school. I understand from your mother that you'll be wearing your cast for at least six weeks, maybe longer. But that's no reason why you can't come to school."

"Yes," agreed Cricket, nodding.

"Here," said Mr. Flores. He reached into his backpack again. "I got this in the mail this afternoon. It was misaddressed, so it arrived too late for me to inform the class about it. But I thought it was something that would interest you."

Cricket glanced down at the two-page notice her teacher handed her.

"The postal system is sponsoring a contest for elementary school students to design a postage stamp showing the importance of caring for our environment. The deadline is April fifteenth. I thought you might like to take a crack at it. It would be a challenge for you to design a stamp," Mr. Flores explained.

"That sounds like fun," Cricket said. "But I'm not very good at drawing."

"Give it a shot," suggested Mr. Flores. "What have you got to lose? I'd be very proud to paste stamps that were designed by one of my students on the letters I write," he said.

"Okay," Cricket said. In any event, it would be something to do during the spring break.

"And one more thing," the teacher said. "I've

saved the best for last," he added, winking at Cricket. He reached into his backpack once again. This time he pulled out a gift-wrapped package.

"Here is a get-well present from the entire class," he said. "We spent some money from the class account. Even though you're vice-president of the class and weren't there to approve the decision, Julio as class president felt it was all right to go ahead. Everyone else agreed too."

Vice-President Cricket Kaufman took the gift from her teacher. "Thank you," she said.

"I want a present too," said Monica. She had been standing with her thumb in her mouth and watching quietly all this time.

"Maybe Cricket will share it with you," said Mr. Flores.

"Do you want to sign my cast?" Cricket offered. She had admitted to Zoe the evening before that she wouldn't be the first to write her name on the cast after all.

"It would be an honor," her teacher said, smiling. He removed his pen from his jacket pocket and bent down. He signed his name in the flowery cursive style that he had. Cricket liked the loops in his name.

"Make the most of your time," Mr. Flores said.

He waved good-bye to Cricket and Monica and went to speak with Mrs. Kaufman before leaving the house. Cricket carefully took the gift wrap off her present. The package rattled mysteriously. Inside were lots of little balls wrapped in foil paper that looked like a map of the world. Cricket removed the foil protecting one of the little globes. It was chocolate.

She stuffed it into her mouth. "Here," she offered Monica as she unwrapped another of the little balls. "One for you and one for me."

Monica put the chocolate inside her mouth instead of her thumb. "More?" she asked, holding out her hand.

Cricket shook her head and closed the box. She was going to be wearing her cast for a long time. If she just had one chocolate ball a day, maybe they would last until the cast was removed.

4
Another Visitor

The weekend passed very slowly. Even though she loved reading, Cricket became restless and bored. She finished one of the library books that Mr. Flores had brought her, but she didn't feel like starting another. Mr. Kaufman went out and rented a couple of videos that Cricket could watch on the VCR. Her mother made a batch of popcorn. It should have been great, but Cricket missed having Zoe sitting by her side and giggling along with her as they watched the films.

She looked at the pages Mr. Flores had given her

about the competition for designing a postage stamp and studied the instructions. The contest was open to all students between the ages of eight and thirteen. Everyone had to depict ways to preserve, protect, restore, or appreciate the environment. Drawings for the contest did not have to be as tiny as a stamp. They could be as big as a sheet of paper eight and a half by eleven inches. Drawings were to be in color, and all entries had to be sent to Washington by April 15. That gave Cricket almost a week to see what she could do.

Since her class had often talked about the environment, Cricket knew a lot about the subject. She took out her markers and stared at a sheet of paper. It would be fantastic to design a postage stamp, she thought. If she won the contest, she would want to write about a hundred letters so she could put the stamp on every one of them. Then she realized that a hundred stamps would cost a lot of money. She wondered if the winner got some of the stamps for free.

Cricket read through the rest of the information about the contest. No. Winners would not get stamps, but they would get a savings bond worth five hundred dollars. Wow! You could buy enough stamps to last your whole life with that much money.

For at least half an hour Cricket tried to draw pictures about the environment. She was not satisfied with any of them. After a while she put her markers away with disgust. Maybe she would try again another day.

On Saturday it had rained all day, but Sunday was bright and sunny. Mrs. Kaufman felt Cricket should get some fresh air, and because she had been able to borrow a wheelchair from the medical center, she told Cricket she would take her for a ride. It was strange to sit in a wheelchair and have her mother push her down the street. Stranger still, little Monica walked alongside Mrs. Kaufman. It was as if suddenly Cricket had become the baby sister in the family.

Neighbors stopped to greet them. "You poor thing," said Mrs. Holden, who was holding the Sunday newspaper.

"I broke my leg once," said Mr. Peaslee. "It seems to me I had to wear that darn cast for six months."

Cricket shuddered. Six months would mean she'd be stuck with the cast all summer long. She'd even be wearing it when she entered sixth grade!

After a while Monica got tired of walking. She climbed up and settled herself on Cricket's lap. Mrs.

Kaufman pushed the two of them together. "This is fun!" Monica exclaimed with delight. She put her thumb in her mouth and leaned back against Cricket.

Cricket's mother found it difficult to push the chair up and down over the curbs. So instead of going any distance, they went back and forth on their street. Before long the novelty of being a passenger in a wheelchair ceased. It was too boring for Cricket. "I've had enough fresh air," she complained. "I'd rather breathe the old air inside the house."

"Tomorrow you can practice walking outdoors with your crutches," Mrs. Kaufman told her daughter.

"Me too," said Monica, taking her thumb out of her mouth. "I want to walk with crushes too."

"I wish Zoe was home," Cricket said crossly. Why did everything happen at the same time: her broken ankle and the departure of her friend? "If Zoe was home, she'd come over and visit me."

"Actually, you're going to have a visitor this afternoon," said Mrs. Kaufman.

"Who?" asked Cricket. "Is Mr. Flores coming back to see me again?" Even as she said it, she remembered that her teacher had told her he was going on a hiking trip.

"No," said her mother, smiling. "It's one of your classmates."

"Oh," said Cricket with disgust. "Lucas Cott. He's probably coming to see if there are any chocolates left."

"It's not Lucas," said Mrs. Kaufman. "I got a call this morning from the mother of a girl in your class."

"Zoe!" Cricket almost stood up in the wheelchair with delight. "Did Zoe come home already? She told me she was going to be away for six days."

"It's not Zoe. And I'm not telling you who it is either," said Cricket's mother. "If I tell you, then it won't be a surprise."

Cricket spent the rest of her ride in the wheelchair and all of her lunchtime speculating. Who could be coming to visit her? She mentally ran down the names of all the girls in her class. But she could not imagine which one would be coming to her house.

When the doorbell rang at two-thirty, Cricket waited eagerly in the living room. She was glad that Monica was still napping. She didn't want her sister to bother her when she had a visitor. To her amazement, who should walk into the room but Sara Jane Cushman?

"Sara Jane!" shrieked Cricket. "What are you doing here? How come you're not in Washington?"

Sara Jane looked down at the floor instead of at Cricket. "I didn't go to Washington," she whispered softly.

"You didn't go?" gasped Cricket. "How come?" Could Zoe have taken back her invitation to Sara Jane at the last minute?

"Well, Zoe invited me, and I thought I was going," said Sara Jane. "I packed my suitcase. I had my new warm-up outfit and a pair of slacks and three shirts and a sweater. I packed my favorite nightgown and my underwear and toothbrush. Everything."

"So what happened?" asked Cricket.

"My mother drove me to Zoe's house first thing yesterday morning. They were going to leave at eight A.M. So I got to her house by seven-thirty. I had to wake up even earlier than on a school day."

"Then what?" Cricket urged Sara Jane to continue.

"Zoe and her sister and another girl were all there talking together and laughing and eating toast. Her father was making jokes, but I didn't understand them. And I began to think about how my father and I make pancakes together every Sunday morning. I was going to miss that."

"But you'd be home on the next Sunday morning," Cricket pointed out.

"It just seemed so far away. I couldn't wait to see my parents for six whole days. I was afraid I'd start crying. So I said I had to go home. I wanted to go with Zoe, but I wanted to go home at the same time. It's hard to explain."

"You were homesick," said Cricket. She'd never had that problem. It was true that she'd never gone away for more than a single evening at a time when she had sleepover dates with Zoe. But she was certain that she would never get homesick.

"Yes," whispered Sara Jane. "I was just like a baby. They had to call my mother, and she was only just coming in the door at my house. Then she had to come back to get me. Zoe begged me to stay. She talked about all the things we could do. But it didn't matter. I just wanted to be sure I'd sleep in my own bed last night."

"Did you and your father make pancakes this morning?" Cricket asked.

Sara Jane nodded.

Poor Sara Jane, Cricket thought. She looked just

as miserable about not going to Washington as Cricket had felt when she broke her ankle. But at least Cricket didn't have to be angry at herself for acting like a baby. She also didn't have to worry anymore about Zoe getting to like Sara Jane better than her. Probably Zoe was furious with Sara Jane for backing out of the trip to Washington.

"Lots of people get homesick," Cricket told Sara Jane. "My mother said she felt homesick for a whole week when she went off to college. Probably by the next time you want to go away, you'll be fine."

"Maybe," said Sara Jane. She smiled shyly at Cricket. "I hope you're right," she added.

"How come you came to visit me?" Cricket asked. She couldn't remember Sara Jane ever coming to her house before.

"Everyone in the class said how terrible it was for you to break your ankle, especially just before spring break. I told my mother about it, and she said maybe I could cheer you up," said Sara Jane. "The only problem is I'm not very good at cheering people up. I don't know how to do it."

"Guess what?" Cricket said, smiling at Sara Jane. "You've cheered me up already."

5

Hot Cupcakes

Sara Jane had brought a gift for Cricket. But what with the surprise of seeing her classmate and then hearing her revelation about her attack of homesickness, Cricket didn't receive the package until Sara Jane was leaving for home.

"My mother helped me pick it out," she whispered shyly as she handed Cricket the present, which had been lying underneath Sara Jane's jacket on one of the living room chairs.

Cricket tore the wrapping paper eagerly. About the only good thing that she had discovered regarding her broken ankle was the unexpected arrival of so many gifts. Inside the package was a plastic envelope with a piece of white linen that had a drawing on it. There were also many colored strands of sewing thread.

"It's called a sampler," Sara Jane explained as Cricket spread out the cloth. Printed on it in big capital letters was *HOME SWEET HOME*. The drawing showed a house surrounded by trees and flowers.

"When you're finished sewing the message and the picture, you can get it framed," said Sara Jane.

Cricket didn't really like sewing at all. Her mother had taught her how to sew the buttons on her clothing when they came off. Cricket had decided that sewing was the world's most boring activity. "It may be dull, but it's essential to know how," Mrs. Kaufman had told Cricket. Cricket didn't think it was *essential* to know how to sew messages on pieces of fabric. But she knew enough to try to be polite. So she pretended to like her gift, and she thanked Sara Jane.

After Sara Jane went home, Cricket looked at her present again. All the words were written with tiny *x*'s. The picture was made with *x*'s too. Sara Jane had explained that it was cross-stitch embroidery. Having already spent so much time reading, Cricket felt like doing something else now. She decided that she'd try sewing just a few stitches on the cloth. It seemed to her that someone in one of the books she'd read had made a cross-stitch sampler. Was it Laura Ingalls in one of the Little House books?

Cricket threaded the needle that came in the package with red thread. She made a knot in the thread the way her mother had taught her and began sewing red *x*'s to make the house. When she got tired of sewing with red thread, she filled in the leaves on one of the trees with green thread.

Cricket was surprised when her mother came to help her into the kitchen to eat supper. The time had passed much more quickly than she had expected. Sewing on the sampler was not nearly as boring as sewing on buttons. It must be because of all the different colored threads, she decided.

Later in the evening Cricket even phoned Sara Jane to tell her how much of the sampler she had completed.

"Would you like me to come and visit you again?" asked Sara Jane shyly.

"Sure," said Cricket. It was better than nothing, since Zoe was away. "Come tomorrow."

"I can't tomorrow," Sara Jane said. "How's Tuesday?"

On Sara Jane's second visit the girls baked cupcakes. It was Mrs. Kaufman's suggestion. Cricket sat on a kitchen chair, and her mother handed her all the needed ingredients. Then Cricket and Sara Jane took turns cracking the eggs and beating in the sugar and the flour.

While they were in the midst of the cupcake preparation, the telephone rang. Mrs. Kaufman wiped her hands on a paper towel and went to answer the phone.

Sara Jane smiled at Cricket. "This is fun," she said. "I like cooking."

"Me too," said Cricket. "It's like we're running our own bakery shop. We could call it Kaufman and Cushman's Bakery."

"Shouldn't it be Cushman and Kaufman?" asked Sara Jane. "That way it would be alphabetical."

"It doesn't need to be alphabetical. And besides, it's my idea and my kitchen where we're cooking," Cricket said authoritatively.

Mrs. Kaufman got off the phone. "That was Mrs. Cott," she said. "She was checking because Lucas and Julio wanted to drop by and visit you again. I told her it would be just fine. The boys will be over in about forty-five minutes."

"That will be fun," said Sara Jane.

Cricket was less sure about that. Even though Lucas's behavior had improved considerably over the past couple of years, she still remembered all the mischief he had gotten into in the past. She didn't always trust the supposedly new and improved Lucas Cott. She was always waiting for him to pull one of his old pranks. As for Julio, Cricket was still a bit jealous that she had lost the class election to him last fall. The fact that he was such a close friend of Lucas's made her suspicious of him too. Who knew what the pair of them was capable of doing?

"I have to go and pick up Monica from her play group," said Mrs. Kaufman. "But the cupcakes will be done, and I'll leave everything out so you can serve them to the boys. It will be like a little tea party for you."

Cricket made a face. Now they'd have to share the cupcakes with Lucas and Julio.

While the cupcakes were baking in the oven, Mrs. Kaufman showed the girls how to make frosting. She melted some butter and added cocoa powder and confectioners' sugar. Both girls stuck their fingers into the mixture. It looked, smelled, and tasted just like fudge.

Cricket's mother set out plates and glasses on the table so that everything would be arranged when the boys arrived. She took the finished cupcakes out of the oven.

"They smell great," said Sara Jane.

"Let the cupcakes cool for about ten minutes," Mrs. Kaufman suggested. "Then you can frost them, and they'll be ready for eating. I have to stop for a few errands on the way back with Monica. But I won't be gone more than an hour or so."

"Okay," said Cricket, smiling. She was hatching a plot and was eager for her mother to leave.

"Have a good time," Mrs. Kaufman said to them both.

After she left, the girls began frosting the cupcakes. Then Cricket turned to Sara Jane. "I have a great idea," she said. "Let's play a joke on Lucas and Julio."

"What kind of joke?" Sara Jane asked.

"We could frost all the cupcakes but leave two of them till the end. Then we could add stuff to the frosting and give those to the boys to eat."

"What kind of stuff?" asked Sara Jane suspiciously.

"Well, pepper, for a start," said Cricket. "I'll need

44

your help. You can look in the cupboard and tell me what else you see."

"Won't it make the cupcakes taste bad?" asked Sara Jane.

"Sure," said Cricket, grinning. "That's the idea. Then they won't want to eat them all up. You know how piggy boys can be."

"It doesn't sound like a nice thing to do," said Sara Jane. "I don't think the Kaufman and Cushman Bakery should make things that taste bad."

"It's just a joke," said Cricket. "Will you help me or won't you?"

"I don't know," said Sara Jane. "I never heard of doing such a thing."

"It won't hurt them. It will just be like a late April Fools' joke," said Cricket. "It's still April, after all. If Zoe was here, she'd help me," she added.

"All right," said Sara Jane reluctantly. She climbed onto the little step stool near the cupboard and began pulling bottles and jars from the shelves. Soon Cricket had a whole assortment in front of her on the table: salt, pepper, crushed red pepper, Worcestershire sauce, soy sauce, mustard powder, and ground ginger.

Cricket remembered the hot horseradish sauce in the refrigerator and made Sara Jane bring that to her as well.

Then she began to pour a bit of everything into the remaining frosting. "The bad cupcakes will look just like the others." Cricket giggled. "But we'll know which ones are which. See? I'm putting the frosting on even thicker than on the other cupcakes. I know those guys. They'll especially want to eat these two."

"It would make me sick," said Sara Jane.

"It'll taste awful, but they won't get sick. Believe me," said Cricket, reassuring her classmate.

They put the cupcakes on a platter and cleared away all the evidence. Sara Jane was just putting the soy sauce and the Worcestershire sauce back into the cupboard when the doorbell rang.

"There they are!" said Cricket with delight. "Let them in. And remember: Act naturally. Don't tell them what we did."

A moment later Sara Jane returned to the kitchen, followed by Lucas and Julio.

"Here's your mail," said Lucas. "I took it out of the box for you." He handed Cricket several envelopes and a magazine. "The top envelope is addressed to you," he pointed out.

Cricket grabbed the envelope. She noticed the postmark said *Washington, D.C.*, and she recognized Zoe's handwriting on the envelope.

"Look," she announced proudly. "Zoe wrote to me, just like she promised." She ripped open the envelope and let out a gasp. There, looking up at her, was a photograph of Zoe, and standing on one side of her was the president of the United States. On the other side was the first lady.

Lucas, Julio, and Sara Jane all crowded around Cricket to get a good look at the photograph.

"Wow!" exclaimed Julio. "Imagine Zoe getting to meet the president!"

"If I was there, I'd have met him too," Cricket reminded her classmates. She thought sadly of her near brush with fame. She looked in the envelope to see if there was a note from Zoe with the picture. It was empty except for the photograph. Cricket turned the photo over. On the back Zoe had written, *The president of the United States and the first lady join me in hoping that your ankle is getting better.*

"Look," said Cricket excitedly. "Even the president of the United States knows about my ankle. If I was in Washington, he could sign my cast."

"Yeah. But you're not, so he can't," Lucas pointed out.

"Don't rub it in," said Cricket. The photograph

from Zoe reminded her once again of the grand opportunity that she had missed.

"Maybe the president wouldn't have wanted to sign your cast anyhow," said Lucas. "He has more important things to do than that."

Cricket began to feel so mad at Lucas that she almost told him to go home. But then she remembered the cupcakes. She'd get back at Lucas as soon as he sampled the baking that she and Sara Jane had done.

Cricket inspected the other envelopes that Lucas had brought into the house. They all were for her parents. "Please put these on the desk in the living room," she asked Julio. "Then you and Lucas can have some milk and cupcakes. Sara Jane and I just baked them."

"Neat," said Julio. "I could smell them when I walked in." He gave an admiring look at the cupcakes. "Chocolate frosting. Yum. I love chocolate," he said. "I picked out your present from the class. Did you like it?"

Cricket nodded. She suspected that Julio was hoping she'd offer him some of the chocolate balls to eat. Well, she wouldn't. Besides, he wouldn't be so keen on chocolate after she was through with him.

Lucas and Julio sat down at the kitchen table.

Sara Jane took the container of milk out of the refrigerator. Cricket placed the two *special* cupcakes on plates and slid them across the table. One for Lucas. One for Julio. Then she took two regular cupcakes and put them on plates for herself and Sara Jane.

"Yum," said Julio, picking up his cupcake. "It's got an extra load of frosting on it too. I didn't know you were such a great cook," he said to Cricket. "I forgot. What did you make for our class bake sale last fall?"

Then, without waiting for an answer to his question, he took a huge bite of the cupcake in his hand.

Cricket watched him. The expression on Julio's face turned from one of great delight to one of shock. He kept on chewing, but he looked very unhappy. Tears even started running down his cheeks. He reached for his glass of milk and took a huge gulp.

Cricket turned to look at Lucas. He too had taken a big bite of cupcake. But unlike Julio, he didn't attempt to swallow what was in his mouth. He spit it out onto his plate. "This is gross," he said. "You can't cook at all. This is the worst cupcake that I ever tasted."

"It's gross of you to spit out food onto your plate," said Cricket.

Julio swallowed the cupcake in his mouth. He looked at the remaining cake in his hand. He took another swallow of milk and then took a tiny bite of his cupcake. "It's very spicy," he said. "It's even making my eyes tear. I never had such hot, spicy chocolate before."

Through it all, Sara Jane sat silently nibbling on her cupcake.

"I think you're trying to poison us," Lucas said. "If anything happens to Julio, you become the class president."

Cricket looked again at Julio. He was bravely trying to finish his cupcake.

"Don't criticize Cricket," Julio said to Lucas. "She and Sara Jane made the best cupcakes they could."

Suddenly Cricket realized what a truly nice guy Julio was. He thought her baking stank, but he didn't want to hurt her feelings.

"Maybe there was something wrong with that cupcake," she suggested. "Here, try another one." She put another cupcake on Julio's plate.

"I don't think I have room for two cupcakes," said Julio. He looked absolutely miserable.

"Please. Don't finish the one you're eating. Please. Try this other one," Cricket begged. She wanted Julio to know that she could really make good cupcakes if she wanted to.

"Here," Cricket added, and she put another cupcake on Lucas's plate too—even though he didn't deserve it.

"I think I'll take this other one home with me," said Julio. "Maybe I'll eat it later."

"I wouldn't let one of your cupcakes into my house," said Lucas. "One of my brothers might get hold of it, and that would be the end of him."

"Please," said Sara Jane softly. "Just take a tiny taste of the new cupcake."

"All right," said Julio. "Just a teeny-tiny taste." He bit off the smallest amount of cupcake possible. He chewed it and looked puzzled. He took another bite, which was a little larger. Then he smiled. "Are all these cupcakes made from the same recipe?" he asked Sara Jane.

Sara Jane looked at Cricket. She didn't know what to say.

"Actually," said Cricket, "there were some different ingredients used in the first cupcake you had. I guess you didn't like that one as much as the second."

"Yeah," Julio said. "Stick with the second recipe

from now on. It's much better." He popped the rest of the second cupcake into his mouth.

"Aren't you going to eat that?" he asked Lucas. He pointed to the untouched second cupcake on his plate.

"No way," said Lucas.

"I'll take it," said Julio, and he polished off his third cupcake.

"Man. You sure like to suffer," said Lucas to Julio as the boys got ready to leave.

Afterward, Cricket and Sara Jane laughed and laughed. Sara Jane was a good sport not to tell about their trick, Cricket thought.

She studied the picture of Zoe and the president of the United States. It had been fun tricking Lucas Cott, but Cricket wished she were in Washington and in the photograph.

6

The Contest

After supper that evening, while studying the photograph that Zoe had sent her, as well as the envelope with its Washington, D.C., postmark, Cricket resolved to try again to make a drawing for the postage stamp competition.

Cricket knew that she had many talents. She was an excellent speller. She was pretty good in math. She read on a very high level and could write good reports. However, when it came to drawing, she was only average. Secretly she worried that maybe she was less than average. Whatever she wanted to draw never came out as well on paper as it did in her imagination.

She remembered what happened once back when she was in first grade. The teacher had read "Cinderella" to the class. Afterward everyone was told to draw a picture of Cinderella in the gown that the fairy godmother had created for her. Cricket knew exactly what the gown looked like. She knew what Cinderella looked like too. But when she finished her picture, she began to cry. Cinderella just didn't look as beautiful as she was supposed to. Ever since then Cricket was aware that no matter how hard she tried, her drawings were not her best achievements.

On the other hand, she reminded herself now, she *was* neat. Her papers were always the neatest in the class. She could print clear, even letters. If her stamp had a message written on it, the letters would be perfect.

Cricket reached for her crutches and made her way to the desk in the living room. She wanted to look at the stamps on the letters inside the desk. Didn't stamps ever have words instead of just pictures? she wondered.

Most of the stamps she saw merely had pictures. But she was thrilled to see a letter with a stamp that had the word *LOVE* on it in big letters. There was another stamp with the word *FLORIDA* in bold letters. Convinced, Cricket called, "Mom, could you bring me the papers on my desk upstairs, and my markers?"

Mrs. Kaufman stopped whatever she had been doing in the kitchen and went to get the papers for Cricket.

"I'm going to try extra hard to design a postage stamp," Cricket explained to her mother. "I might win a five-hundred-dollar savings bond."

"That would be great!" said Mrs. Kaufman. "But even if you don't win, I think it would be fun for you to try to design a stamp."

Cricket spread her papers and markers out on the kitchen table. Then she started writing. *Save our environment,* she printed. Her letters were neat, but it looked boring. She tried to color in the background with green, but it blurred her letters. She realized she should have done the background first and the letters afterward.

Cricket reached for another sheet and started to color it green.

"I want to draw too," said Monica, coming into the room and seeing Cricket at work.

"You can't draw. You only know how to do

scribble-scrabble," said Cricket.

"I can draw. Can't I?" Monica asked her mother.

The problem with Monica was that she had a huge vocabulary for a girl of her age. But she really couldn't do all the things she saw Cricket doing.

"Of course you can draw," said Mrs. Kaufman. She winked at Cricket. "Give Monica a piece of paper," she said.

"I need a marker too," Monica pointed out. "Purple," she specified.

Cricket sighed, but she handed over the purple marker. Usually she was proud that Monica knew all her colors. Cricket had taught them to her. Luckily Cricket wasn't planning to use the purple marker herself.

Monica scribbled all over the sheet of paper that Cricket gave her. Then she reached for another sheet and scribbled over that one too.

Cricket looked down on her own piece of paper. Maybe she could think of a better message. She made a list of messages:

> Keep our water clean
> Don't waste anything
> Protect the earth
> Pure water tastes best

Recycle
Stop pollution

It suddenly occurred to Cricket that her messages were like the words on her sampler. Even *Home Sweet Home* could mean that there wasn't waste and pollution at home. Cricket reached for a new sheet of paper.

She drew a picture of a house surrounded by trees. The sun was shining, and grass grew on the ground. Above the house she wrote *Home Sweet Home.* It was a simple scene, clear and bold, just the way it should be on a stamp.

"I made more pictures than you," Monica bragged. She had a whole pile of papers covered with purple lines.

"That's great," said Cricket, hardly paying attention. A thought had just struck her. She took another sheet of paper, and instead of drawing a picture, she made the outline of a map of the United States. Of course, it didn't include Alaska and Hawaii, but everyone would know what she meant. Inside the map Cricket printed the words *Home Sweet Home.*

Another idea came to Cricket. Instead of drawing her map with straight lines, she could draw it using tiny x's. Then it would look just like the sampler that Sara Jane had given her.

"Hang my pictures up," Monica demanded of her mother.

"They are wonderful. But I can't hang all of them," Mrs. Kaufman said. "There are too many. You'd better pick two of your favorites."

Cricket watched as Monica selected two of her purple scribbles. Then Mrs. Kaufman attached them with small magnets to the side of the refrigerator.

Monica went off with her mother to get ready for bed. But Cricket continued working at her stamp design. She worked slowly and intently. X by x she covered the outline of the United States. Using only x's, she wrote out the words *Home Sweet Home*. It took twelve tiny x's just to make the first H in the word *Home*. But it was worth the effort. When she completed her design, she looked at it with pride. For once she hadn't imagined something more beautiful inside her head. This looked exactly the way she had hoped it would.

"Cricket, that's lovely," Mrs. Kaufman complimented her daughter. "And very clever too."

"It would make a great stamp," her father said.

"Do you really mean it?" Cricket asked. Parents sometimes seemed to feel that they had to say certain things to make their kids feel good. After all, her mother had just admired Monica's purple scribbles.

"Absolutely," said Mr. Kaufman. "Mail it off exactly as it is. I think it's perfect."

Cricket beamed. "Do you think I'll win the contest?" she asked. "There are going to be four winners," she told her parents.

"I'll keep my fingers crossed," said Mrs. Kaufman. Then she laughed. "Like the crosses on your design."

Cricket looked among the papers on the table for the page with the contest rules. She couldn't find it. "Could you look for the rules for me? Maybe they're still on my desk upstairs."

"Sure," said Mr. Kaufman, and he went up to Cricket's room.

In a few minutes he returned without the rules. "I can't find them," he said. "When you go upstairs to bed, you can look yourself."

After her first couple of nights of sleeping on the living room sofa, Cricket had returned to her bedroom upstairs. Her father carried her up in the evening and down again in the morning. Later, upstairs in her room, Cricket looked among all the papers on her desk. She looked in the wastebasket; she looked among the papers in her backpack; she looked under her bed.

"I don't know where the rules are," she complained to her mother when she came to tuck Cricket into bed.

"I'm sure they'll turn up," said Mrs. Kaufman.

"What if they don't?" Cricket worried aloud.

"Maybe I can phone the local post office and see if they know anything about the contest."

"That's a good idea," Cricket said.

The next morning Mrs. Kaufman kept her word. She called the post office for information. Unfortunately no one on the staff knew anything about an art contest for schoolchildren.

"Don't worry," Mrs. Kaufman said to Cricket. She went upstairs to Cricket's room and looked through everything. She even spread newspaper out on the kitchen floor and dumped out all the garbage in the pail. Cricket watched anxiously, and Monica watched with amazement. This was something that had never been done before in their kitchen. Among the garbage there were grapefruit halves, coffee grinds, carrot scrapings, an empty cardboard orange juice container, a bread wrapper, eggshells, wet tea bags, and the packaging from frozen peas. There were even several discarded purple drawings of Monica's. But there was no sign of the contest rules.

As the day passed, Mrs. Kaufman kept getting new ideas. "Did you use the pages as a bookmark?" she asked. Cricket shook her head no. Still, Mrs. Kaufman went to examine the pile of library books.

Cricket admired her design sadly. It seemed the worst possible luck that she had managed to make such a good stamp but had lost the contest rules. She remembered that it had to be mailed by April 15. But she didn't know where to mail it. This was April 13.

"I've got another idea," said Mrs. Kaufman when she saw Cricket looking at her stamp design. "I'll phone the administrative office of the Board of Education. Just because school is closed doesn't mean that the offices won't be open."

"Oh, what a great idea," Cricket said, smiling. She was lucky that her mother was so smart. She probably got a lot of her own smartness from her, just as she had gotten her mother's straight brown hair.

Mrs. Kaufman looked in the telephone book for the number, then called the office. Cricket held her breath. Would someone answer the phone?

Mrs. Kaufman stood holding the telephone. It

must have rung several times, because she didn't say anything. Then Cricket's mother spoke. "Hello," she said. "I'm trying to find out some information about a contest for children in elementary school that the post office is running.

"All right," said Mrs. Kaufman after a brief pause. She put her hand over the mouthpiece of the phone and reported to Cricket, "The woman is transferring my call to someone who may be able to help us."

Several seconds passed. Then Mrs. Kaufman repeated her request. "All right," she said again. "I'm being transferred to another department," she explained to Cricket.

In all, Cricket's mother spoke to four different people at the Board of Education. None of them knew anything about the contest.

"Well, we tried," said Mrs. Kaufman when she hung up the phone.

Cricket nodded sadly. It didn't look as if she'd be able to enter the contest after all.

"Think about something else," suggested her mother. "Maybe the location of that sheet of paper will just pop into your head when you least expect it."

"Yeah. But there isn't very much time," Cricket complained. There wasn't much to distract her today. Sara Jane had gone shopping with her mother. Lucas and Julio had told Cricket that they were going to play with their Little League team that day. So Cricket sat wondering what the use of her beautiful entry was if she didn't know how to enter the contest.

7

In the Middle of the Night

By bedtime Cricket's mood had gone from bad to worse. She hadn't wanted to read a story to Monica and had yelled at her little sister to stop nagging her. She hadn't wanted to play cards with her father when he offered to entertain her. She hadn't wanted to try to help her mother with the crossword puzzle though some days she surprised both her mother and herself by figuring out some of the answers. She hadn't even wanted to watch television.

Inside the cast her leg itched. Her head ached

too. It was probably hurting from thinking so much about the contest.

Mr. Kaufman picked up Cricket and carried her upstairs. "Get a good night's sleep," he told her. "Tomorrow is another day. Maybe things will be better."

"How can they possibly be better?" Cricket demanded in a grumpy voice. "I'll still have a broken ankle tomorrow."

"Yes, but isn't Zoe due back home?" he asked her.

Somehow Cricket had actually forgotten that the next day was when Zoe was returning. Instead of making her feel good, it only reminded her of her missed opportunity to visit Washington. "She'll just want to talk about her trip," Cricket complained.

"That's true. But if you had gone to Washington, your mother and I would have listened to you talk about it. I should think you'd want to hear your friend talk about her trip."

"It's not the same," said Cricket. An angry thought came into her head: Parents just didn't understand.

Cricket got out of her clothes and into her nightgown. She made her way into the bathroom and washed her face and brushed her teeth.

"Do you want to read in bed for a little while?"

asked Mrs. Kaufman, who had come upstairs. Since it was vacation time, her parents were letting her stay up extra late these past few days.

"I don't feel like reading," whined Cricket. "I read all afternoon."

"All right," said her mother. "Get a good night's sleep. And tomorrow try to get out of bed on the right side." One side of Cricket's bed was against the wall, but she knew what her mother meant. She really meant that Cricket should be in a better mood. It was easy for her to say that. She hadn't broken her ankle or missed a vacation trip or made a wonderful contest entry that she couldn't submit because she'd lost the address.

Cricket got into bed, accidentally hitting the leg with the cast against the side of her bed. Her mother leaned over to give Cricket a kiss.

Two little tears squeezed out of Cricket's eyes. "Cheer up," Mrs. Kaufman said, kissing Cricket a second time. "Maybe something good will happen tomorrow."

"Nothing good can happen tomorrow," said Cricket as her mother turned out the light. She felt absolutely miserable.

It seemed like forever until Cricket fell asleep. She tossed and turned in bed even though tossing and turning were not easy with the heavy cast on her leg. But eventually she must have fallen asleep, because she had a dream. In her dream she was standing in the kitchen and serving homemade cookies to Julio and Lucas.

"Do you want more?" she asked the boys.

"I'm starving," said Julio. "I love the way you cook. I could eat everything in your refrigerator."

"Me too," said Lucas.

Cricket opened the refrigerator and started taking everything out. She ran back and forth, piling the food on the kitchen table.

"What funny pictures you drew," said Lucas, pointing to the artwork hanging on the refrigerator.

"I didn't draw those," said Cricket. She pulled one of the pictures down and held it out. Lucas was just about to take the picture out of Cricket's hand when she woke up. For a moment Cricket lay in bed thinking of her dream. It was funny the way she had loaded the table with all the food in the refrigerator. She had even taken out uncooked items like eggs and a package of raw chicken parts. She didn't think she was wearing a cast in her dream, because she was able to get around easily. She wondered what had woken her. Suddenly she knew.

In the dream she had pulled one of Monica's

pictures off the refrigerator to show the boys. On the back of the paper were the contest rules. She was certain that if she looked at the papers that Monica had scribbled on, one of them would have the rules on the reverse side.

It was still the middle of the night, but Cricket couldn't wait until morning. She had to go check right away. She sat up in her bed. For a moment she thought about calling out for her parents. Monica still woke her parents at least once a week. If she woke her father, he could carry her downstairs. But suppose she was wrong. That would be embarrassing. Cricket decided she would make the trip downstairs on her own.

She couldn't use her crutches on the stairs. But she could go down on her bottom. That's the way Monica had gone downstairs when she was little. Cricket got out of bed and sat on the floor. She wished she had turned on the light by her bed, but it was too late now. She started crawling toward the door in the dark.

Her door was half open, so she made her way out into the upstairs hallway. The rug felt itchy on her legs, but she kept moving. She felt with her hands and found the top stair. She sat with her legs dangling down and pulled herself down one stair. It wasn't too hard. Then she went down another and another.

Finally she reached the bottom step. She sat for a moment catching her breath. Now she could have used her crutches. She knew they were somewhere in the living room, where she had left them. But she didn't want to waste time looking for them. Instead she held on to the nearest piece of furniture, her father's armchair. She pulled herself up. Then she reached out for the next piece and hopped toward it.

She was so excited she could hardly wait to reach the kitchen. She knew her parents would be very surprised if they could see her now. There was a lamp to the left of her father's chair, but Cricket was already headed away from it. She was eager to go directly toward the kitchen.

Hopping and holding on to furniture pieces and the wall, Cricket gradually made her way to the kitchen. Now she had to turn a light on. She hopped toward the light switch.

"Ouch!" she shouted aloud as she hit a toe on her good foot against the leg of one of the kitchen chairs. For the first time since she had started her journey from upstairs, and for the first time in several days, she thought again about Helen Keller. It wasn't easy being blind. That was certain!

Suddenly a light came on in the living room, and there were voices.

"Who's there?" Cricket asked anxiously.

"That's what we want to know," said her father's voice. "I didn't really think there was a burglar down here. But there certainly were some very strange noises."

"Are you hungry?" asked Cricket's mother. She was wearing her bathrobe and standing next to her husband, who was clad in his pajamas.

"No," said Cricket, laughing. "But I just woke up from a dream, and I suddenly figured out where the contest rules are." She reached out and grabbed Monica's two drawings. She turned them over. There were the two pages of instructions for entering the postage stamp contest.

Cricket grabbed for the nearest kitchen chair and sat down. Then she looked at the papers with delight.

"That's amazing!" said Mrs. Kaufman, taking the pages from her daughter and studying them. "They were right here in front of us all day long."

"Whatever made you think of it?" asked her father.

"It was Lucas Cott," said Cricket. "He was in my dream, and he asked me about these drawings."

"Imagine Lucas helping you find the missing rules," said Mrs. Kaufman. "He certainly is a good friend. He'll be very surprised to find out what he did, even if it was in a dream."

"Oh, no," gasped Cricket. "Whatever you do, don't tell Lucas that I dreamed about him." Cricket knew she would never be able to live that down.

"All right," agreed her mother.

"Can you get me an envelope?" Cricket asked.

"An envelope? At three-thirty in the morning?" asked Mr. Kaufman.

"For my contest entry," Cricket explained. "I need a stamp too."

"Tomorrow morning," said Mrs. Kaufman firmly.

"It *is* tomorrow morning," Cricket pointed out.

"It's the middle of the night too," said Mr. Kaufman. "Hold tight to those rules. Don't lose them again." Then he picked his daughter up and carried her back upstairs.

So Cricket found herself back in bed. "I guess I got out on the right side," she told her mother. She closed her eyes and wondered if she would have another dream starring Lucas Cott.

8

Surprises from Zoe

On Friday morning of spring break, Cricket got a phone call at eight in the morning. She was awake, but still in her nightgown, and she hadn't eaten breakfast yet either. It was the earliest she had ever spoken on the phone. The call was from Zoe Mitchell.

"I got home too late to call you last night," Zoe said. "I hope I didn't wake you."

"No," said Cricket. "I've been up for ages. I was reading in bed," she admitted.

"Good," said Zoe. "Can I come over after

breakfast? I can't wait to see you. I want to tell you all about Washington, and I have some presents for you too."

"Come as soon as you can. And ask your mother if you can stay for lunch too," Cricket added. "I'm sure it will be okay with my mom. I want to hear about everything. Every single thing you saw and did." Now that Cricket had mailed her contest entry, she was more interested in hearing about Zoe's experiences than she had been before.

"I'll ask my dad to drop me off on his way to work," said Zoe.

Cricket hung up the telephone in her parents' bedroom and hobbled with her crutches back into her room. She'd have to hurry if she wanted to be washed and dressed and finished with breakfast before Zoe arrived. Everything, except eating, took so long to do with her ankle in a cast.

When Zoe arrived an hour later, Cricket was dressed in a skirt and sweater. Her mother had cut the right foot off several of her tights so she could put them on over her cast. When Zoe walked in the door wearing jeans, Cricket looked at her enviously. She couldn't wear jeans or slacks until the cast came off her ankle. The leg hole was too narrow for her cast to fit through. These days she could wear only the stretchy cotton knit pants from her warm-up outfit.

Mrs. Kaufman welcomed Zoe. "Cricket is so happy that you're home again," she said as she zipped up Monica's jacket. Cricket's little sister was just going off to her play group.

"What's in there?" asked Monica.

Zoe was holding a paper shopping bag. "This is for you," she said to Cricket. "It's filled with Washington souvenirs."

"This has something for a big girl. Nothing for you," Cricket told Monica as she took the bag from Zoe.

Mrs. Kaufman quickly distracted Monica before she could protest. "Wave bye-bye," she told her younger daughter.

Cricket sat at the kitchen table with the shopping bag. Inside there were many little packages. "This is like having a birthday!" said Cricket happily. It was better to have many little surprises than one big one.

In a little while the kitchen table was covered with wrapping paper and all the little gifts. There was a package of freeze-dried ice cream, which Zoe said the astronauts ate in space, and a package with a type of candy that people ate in colonial America.

There was a key ring with a reproduction of the Lincoln Memorial, and there was a small book about the history of Washington, D.C. There was a collection of postcards that opened like an accordion. Each card showed another important site in Washington, like the Vietnam War Memorial and the White House and the Library of Congress.

"I didn't mail them because I got home before the cards would have gotten here," Zoe explained.

There was also a small packet of notecards with reproductions of paintings in the National Gallery, and there was a little doll whose body was made out of a turkey wishbone.

"I know we're too old to play with dolls." Zoe giggled. "But I figured this doll was kind of like history. It's a copy of a doll that girls had during the eighteenth century. I got one for myself. Even Halley and Lyndsey bought them."

"It's darling," said Cricket, admiring the calico fabric that the doll's dress and bonnet were made out of. She peeked underneath the doll's long skirt to see her wishbone legs. "Lucky thing. She doesn't have ankles," she said, pointing to the ends of the doll's legs.

"If you had wishbone legs, you couldn't walk," said Zoe. "But you could make a lot of wishes."

"Thank you, thank you, thank you," said Cricket, pointing to each of the items in the box. "I bet you had an absolutely, totally, wonderfully fabulous time in Washington," she said. "Tell me about everything. Tell me about meeting the president first. Was he nice? What did you say to him?"

"The president?" asked Zoe, looking puzzled.

"Yes. The president of the United States? Who do you think I mean?" asked Cricket. "He looks so friendly in the picture. Not serious, the way he always looks on TV."

"The president of the United States? I didn't meet the president of the United States," said Zoe. "The rooms we saw at the White House are just special rooms that are open to the public. They don't let people go into the area where the president actually lives."

"But what about the picture you sent?" Cricket asked. "It's upstairs in my room. You're standing right next to the president and his wife. Where was that picture taken? And didn't you talk to him at all?"

"Oh," said Zoe, starting to laugh. "*That* picture." She laughed so hard that tears began to fall down her cheeks.

"What's so funny?" asked Cricket. "It's a great honor to have a picture taken with the president. I don't know why you think it's a joke."

"Because it *is* a joke," said Zoe, trying hard to catch her breath. "I didn't meet the president. I had my picture taken standing by two cardboard statues. They were flat as boards. Because they are boards." She gasped and started laughing all over again.

"You mean you didn't really meet the president?" asked Cricket.

"No," said Zoe, wiping her eyes. "I could have had my picture taken standing next to the queen of England or the pope or loads of other cardboard people."

Cricket sat trying to decide how to react. She was embarrassed that she had mistaken a cardboard figure for the real person. Sara Jane and Lucas and Julio had thought it was really the president in the picture too. But if Zoe hadn't met the president, then it meant that Cricket hadn't missed out on that chance of a lifetime. It was a chance that hadn't occurred at all.

Cricket smiled at Zoe. "You really fooled me," she said.

Zoe grinned. "I never even thought you'd think it was the real thing," she admitted.

"It's hard for me to go up and down stairs," said Cricket. "I put your card on the bulletin board in my room. Would you go up and get it? I want to study it again now that I know you're not really standing by the president."

Zoe ran up the stairs and returned with the infamous picture.

"Are you sure that this is really you?" asked Cricket, pointing to the image of Zoe. "Maybe you're made out of cardboard also."

"It may not be the president and his wife, but it's the real me," said Zoe, laughing. "I had a great time. But I missed you and I'm glad to be back. Tell me about you. What have you been doing all during the spring break? Was it terribly boring and awful?"

Cricket thought for a minute before she answered. "I don't recommend breaking an ankle. It really limits what you can do," she said. "But you know, I've actually had some fun, even though I was stuck at home." And she began filling Zoe in on what she'd been doing over the past few days.

9

Mr. Flores Is Speechless

Not one student at Edison–Armstrong could have looked forward to returning to school after the spring break as much as Cricket. Vacations always seemed too long to her. But this time she was especially eager to return to school. She'd surprised herself by having more fun at home than she would have ever guessed possible. She'd gotten to know Sara Jane Cushman better, and she was proud of both the sampler she had almost finished sewing and the contest entry she had mailed off.

But now she was ready to return to school. Even more important, she wanted to show off her invalid status to her schoolmates.

Of course everyone in her homeroom class knew she had broken her ankle. But except for the four who had visited her at home—Sara Jane, Lucas, Julio, and Zoe—none of them had yet had a chance to admire the plaster cast on her right leg. They hadn't seen her crutches or the wheelchair. Furthermore, if she came to class with crutches, everyone in the whole school would get to see her. She would certainly be the center of attention. And there was nothing Cricket loved more than being the center of attention!

On the Monday morning that school reopened, Cricket's father drove her to the old brick building. First he helped her get into the car. Then he put her crutches in the backseat. When they arrived at the school, he helped Cricket out of the car and handed her the crutches. Slowly, using the crutches, Cricket walked toward the school's front door. Her father walked beside her carrying her backpack.

Mr. Kaufman had brought Cricket to school very early because he had to continue on to work. They were so early that there were no students around yet to see Cricket walking with crutches and wearing a big white cast on her right leg. Even the teachers didn't seem to have arrived yet, thought Cricket as they approached the entrance to the school.

Fortunately the custodian had unlocked the doors to the building. Cricket didn't think she'd ever been to school so early. She was sorry that there was no one in the halls to see her. But she knew her classmates would be surprised to come into the room and find her already there. Maybe they thought she'd still be absent!

Luckily Cricket's classroom was on the first floor. But Cricket knew that if she'd been up on the second floor, her father would have managed to get her upstairs anyhow.

Even though it was so early, when they got to the classroom there was Mr. Flores sitting behind his desk and busily writing. He looked up and smiled when he saw them. Then he handed a piece of paper to Mr. Kaufman. Cricket's father read the words on the paper and passed it on to his daughter.

I have a bad case of laryngitis. I can't say a word.

"You mean you aren't going to talk today?" Cricket asked her teacher after she had read the note too.

Mr. Flores nodded.

"How can you teach us?" asked Cricket. She'd never heard of a teacher not talking in the classroom. It was impossible!

Mr. Flores wrote a note on another piece of paper. *Today the students will do the talking,* he wrote.

"That will be terrible," said Cricket. "You'd better get a sub for us."

Cricket didn't particularly enjoy it when there was a substitute teacher in the classroom. But she couldn't imagine how Mr. Flores expected to conduct the class if he couldn't talk. Sometimes when there was a sub, the class went really wild. Once, back in third grade, a sub had screamed and screamed at them. The louder she yelled, the worse the students behaved. Cricket had sat primly in her seat, behaving perfectly and having a wonderful time watching the others act up. If Mr. Flores couldn't tell the students how to behave today, they might treat him the same way. It would be awful. She liked Mr. Flores, and she didn't want to see him in such a position.

"Well, good luck," said Mr. Kaufman, shaking hands with Cricket's teacher. "I must say you're very devoted to come to school under these circumstances."

Mr. Flores smiled and shrugged.

"Your mother will be here to pick you up at the end of the day," Mr. Kaufman told Cricket as she got into her seat. She sat on the aisle, so there was room to rest her crutches on the floor. Cricket's father leaned down and kissed the top of her head.

Cricket removed her jacket. Mr. Flores took it from her and hung it in the wardrobe. Then he went to the chalkboard and began writing.

Welcome back from vacation. I had a great time hiking and camping in the woods. Unfortunately it rained the last three days. I caught a cold, which is now better. However, I have lost my voice. I need your total cooperation. I have confidence that we can manage.

Cricket read the message twice. She tried to imagine Mr. Flores out hiking in the rain. It must have been cold. At night it was probably wet inside the tent where he slept. She shuddered. She would have hated that. Why hadn't Mr. Flores just gone home if it was raining? Then he wouldn't have gotten sick.

Cricket opened her notebook and began writing a message to her teacher. Then she started laughing. "For a minute I forgot that even if you can't talk, you can still hear me," she said.

Mr. Flores grinned.

"I entered that postage stamp contest," she told

him. "I think I made a really good design."

Mr. Flores smiled and gave Cricket the thumbs-up sign.

"They won't announce the winner for a few weeks," Cricket said. "But I have my fingers crossed."

Mr. Flores held up his hand and showed that his fingers were crossed too.

It was kind of fun to talk to him this way. But Cricket still had serious doubts that it would work when there was a whole roomful of students.

They began to hear people walking in the hallway. Mr. Flores turned back to the board and wrote: *I will select students to lead each area of study today.*

"Ohhhh." Cricket called out eagerly to her teacher. "Can I be one of the people you pick? I could teach anything."

Mr. Flores smiled at Cricket, but of course he didn't say anything.

Arthur Lewis walked into the classroom, followed by Anne Crosby. They both greeted their teacher. Mr. Flores smiled at them and pointed to the board.

"Wow!" said Arthur. "This is really going to be a weird day if you don't talk to us."

"I think we should get a sub," Cricket told Arthur.

"Oh, no. Forget subs. We never learn anything when we have a sub," said Anne.

"How are we going to learn anything today?" Cricket wanted to know.

More students came into the room. They greeted one another.

"Look at the board," Cricket instructed them.

Everyone was amazed by the words their teacher had written.

"You lost your voice?" Lucas called out to the teacher. "Did you look under rocks and behind the trees for it?"

The students laughed. It was a typical Lucas Cott kind of joke.

Cricket foresaw a day of disaster ahead of them.

Gradually the room filled up. Zoe came in and waved to Cricket as she took her seat. Sara Jane smiled at Cricket shyly. But the students were so busy taking in the unique situation of a teacher without a voice that no one paid much attention to Cricket. It was as if she and her cast and crutches were invisible.

Soon everyone was in the room and talking. Mr. Flores went over to the wall and flicked the light switch. It was always a signal for class attention, and it worked today too. Cricket was relieved about that.

When the room was silent, Mr. Flores erased his message and wrote a new one. *This is a big experiment. I know you are up to it. Don't let me down.*

"We'll be on our best behavior today," said Julio, standing up at his seat. "You can count on us," he promised Mr. Flores.

The teacher gave a big smile to Julio and then looked around and smiled at everyone.

I went camping in the rain, he wrote. *How did you spend your spring break?*

He pointed to Arthur Lewis.

"I went to visit my aunt and uncle and cousins in Pennsylvania. They live on a farm and raise hogs."

Everyone laughed at the thought of Arthur spending his vacation visiting hogs. "Did they smell?" Lucas Cott called out.

"No. I learned a lot about them. And hogs are actually very clean animals."

"Yeah, sure," said Lucas sarcastically.

Mr. Flores walked over to Lucas and patted him on the shoulder.

"Oops. Sorry," said Lucas. "I won't call out again," he promised the teacher. He put his hand across his mouth to show he meant what he said.

Mr. Flores went up and down the rows, pointing to one student after another. Zoe told about going to Washington. Of course Cricket knew all the details of that trip. Lucas told about Little League starting up and how he was going to be a catcher this year. Sara Jane said, "I almost went to Washington with Zoe. But I didn't. Instead I stayed home. And I visited with Cricket. We had a good time together."

Everyone turned to look at Cricket. "You almost went to Washington too," said Lucas, forgetting his promise not to call out.

Mr. Flores pointed to Cricket, indicating that it was her turn to tell the class what she had done during the spring break. "My spring break started earlier than everyone else's," Cricket said. She meant that she had been out of school two extra days.

Everyone laughed at her words. It took Cricket a moment to realize that her broken ankle was a type of spring break too.

"Mostly I stayed home and read and did quiet things that I could do sitting down. The most interesting thing I did was enter a special contest to design a postage stamp. Mr. Flores got the information about the contest too late to tell the whole class about it, but at least he was able to tell me."

As she spoke, Cricket realized for the first time

that she could have shared the information about the contest with Sara Jane and Zoe. Even Lucas and Julio might have wanted to enter the contest if she'd told them about it. She pushed that disquieting thought out of her mind. Sara Jane wasn't as good a student as Cricket, but she was good at drawing. At least now Cricket wouldn't have to compete with her in the contest.

All the students were impressed with Cricket's announcement.

"I bet you win," Arthur Lewis called out.

Cricket blushed. She hoped Arthur was right. "There're going to be *four* winners," she said. "So that makes the chances of winning better."

When everyone had finished telling about vacation, it was time to begin real work. Mr. Flores selected Zoe to lead the class in a review of their math work. Zoe stood in front of the room, just like a teacher. "Open your workbooks to page ninety-seven," she instructed. She copied the problem onto the board. Then she explained how she got her answer.

Cricket would have liked to be standing in Zoe's place. But she realized it would have been impossible for her to turn to the board and back to the class with the ease that Zoe had. It would be difficult, if not impossible, to stand balanced with her crutches and still be able to write on the board. It just wasn't fair that her teacher got laryngitis at a time when she was helpless with a broken ankle. And it wasn't fair that they all were so occupied with the thoughts of having a speechless teacher that they weren't paying much attention to her.

In the middle of the morning Mr. Herbertson opened the door and walked into the classroom. "I came to see how you're managing without a voice," he told Mr. Flores.

Mr. Flores smiled at the principal.

I have a great class, he wrote on the board. *100% cooperation.*

"Wonderful," said Mr. Herbertson. "That's the way it should always be." He looked around the room as if checking on the accuracy of Mr. Flores's statement. Then he nodded to the class and departed.

At three o'clock, when Mrs. Kaufman came to pick up Cricket, the class was quietly packing up their books and papers. "How are you feeling?" Mrs. Kaufman asked Mr. Flores. "I spoke with my husband on the phone, and he told me about your laryngitis."

Mr. Flores smiled at Cricket's mother. He wrote

on the board, *Today I discovered that a teacher doesn't need a voice if he has an A-1 class like mine.*

The students smiled proudly at one another.

Give yourselves a round of applause, Mr. Flores wrote.

Everyone began clapping.

"Do you think you'll be able to talk tomorrow?" asked Lucas.

Mr. Flores shrugged.

The bell rang for dismissal. Usually Mr. Flores called the students by rows to line up. Today he didn't have a voice, so Lucas jumped out of his seat and rushed to leave the room.

Mr. Flores put his fingers to his mouth and gave an amazingly loud whistle. Lucas stopped in his tracks, stunned.

Mr. Flores pointed to Lucas's seat. Lucas knew what that meant and sat down.

Then the teacher began pointing to the various rows to line up. Cricket and her mother waited until everyone in the class had gone. Then Mrs. Kaufman picked up Cricket's crutches and handed them to her.

"That was a great whistle," Cricket called out to her teacher. "I guess your laryngitis didn't affect it." The loud and unexpected whistle was actually like a secret weapon that the teacher had had all day long. But he hadn't needed to use it until Lucas tried to run out of the room at the end of the day.

Mr. Flores smiled at Cricket. Then he nodded to Lucas that he could go home.

"Hey, Mrs. Kaufman? Can I get a ride with you?" Lucas asked.

Cricket made a face, but her mother didn't seem to notice.

"Of course, Lucas," she said.

Silently Cricket crossed her fingers that Lucas would behave in the car. After all, her mother didn't know how to make one of those ear-piercing whistles that would stop Lucas when he got too wild.

10

A Shoe on Each Foot

In only two days Mr. Flores regained the full use of his voice. Classwork resumed its former pattern, with the teacher leading discussions and speaking to his students. But Class 5-F was proud of itself. The students had proved to the whole school what a great group they were. They were a class that could be managed and taught by a teacher without a voice.

It was to take Cricket another five weeks until she regained the full use of her right ankle. She continued receiving rides to school from her father and rides home from her mother. During the day in school she sat reading a library book when her classmates were taking phys ed. She stayed inside the lunchroom during recess, listening to the voices and shouts of the kids outside playing ball and running about in the schoolyard.

At first Cricket felt important and thought it was fun to be in such a special situation. But the novelty quickly wore off. Three days after spring break ended, Cricket found herself feeling full of self-pity. Would life ever return to the way it had been before?

Some days as she sat in the lunchroom while Mr. Conners, the school custodian, swept and mopped up all around her, she distracted herself by thinking of the contest she had entered. She wondered when the winners would be notified. And *how* would they be notified? Would letters be mailed to the homes of the winners? Or would they be sent to their schools? There had been instructions that all entries should include the school name and address and even telephone number. Would they phone the Edison-Armstrong School with the news that Cricket Kaufman was one of the four national winners of the postage stamp contest? The thought of such a call gave

Cricket a shiver of delight.

Cricket relived this daydream on many different occasions. Sometimes she imagined herself sitting in class and Mr. Herbertson walking in the door with the big news. She knew her classmates would be impressed if that happened. Sometimes she thought there would be a letter waiting for her when she got home from school. Then she'd have to wait until the next day to tell everyone the news. (Though of course she would phone Zoe and Sara Jane at once!) Sometimes Cricket had to remind herself that it was also possible that she wouldn't be a winner after all. The thought of such a disappointment was so unpleasant that Cricket didn't like to think about it.

"Hey, Cricket. Did you win that contest yet?" Julio asked her every couple of days.

Then the other kids in their class echoed his question.

"Did you win?"

"When will you hear?"

"What's the prize for the winner?"

I probably should never have told them about it, Cricket thought. She realized it would be absolutely mortifying if she didn't win. If she hadn't announced to her classmates that she'd entered the contest, they would never have known if she didn't win. Too bad. It was too late to retract her comments.

Cricket tried to put the thought out of her head. After all, summer vacation was gradually approaching. Perhaps school would be over before she heard the contest results.

On May 25 Mrs. Kaufman took Cricket for one of her occasional appointments at the orthopedist's office. She had visited several times during the past few weeks, but that day was a special one. The cast, which had started out pristine white, now had a gray tinge. Some of the signatures had blurred because they had not been written with waterproof markers, and even though she used plastic to wrap her cast, moisture had managed to seep through when she took showers.

There was a pinkish area on the cast too. That was from the day that Monica had knocked over Cricket's glass of tomato juice. The cold red liquid had landed on the cast and on the toes peeking out. The toes were washed, but the cast could only be patted a bit with paper towels. So by May 25 the whole cast was looking pretty grungy.

When Dr. Schertle ("It rhymes with turtle," he reminded Cricket, as he had on each of her visits) announced that this was the day he was going to remove her cast, Cricket was thrilled.

Dr. Schertle had a small vibrating saw that he used to cut away the plaster.

"Hold still." The doctor teased Cricket. "You don't want me to cut off your leg by mistake."

Cricket knew he was joking.

"Then you'd just have to sew it back on," she told him.

"*So* I would," said Dr. Schertle, and he chuckled at the pun he had made.

It had been so long since Cricket had put her full weight on her right foot that she was almost scared to do it. Luckily Dr. Schertle gave her a special support to wear over the next week. He called it an air brace. It covered only her ankle and closed with Velcro fasteners, so now she could wear regular clothes and shoes again.

"You're going to have to take it easy for the next few weeks," Dr. Schertle told her. "No jumping rope or Rollerblading."

"What can I do?" asked Cricket.

"Return the crutches and the wheelchair to the medical center. Go for a walk with your friends."

"Walk home from school," suggested Mrs. Kaufman. Cricket guessed her mother was tired of having to make the trip to pick her up every single day.

The part of Cricket's leg that had been covered by the cast was a different shade from the rest of her body. It was pale and sickly looking, like something out of a ghost story. Cricket rubbed her leg with her hand. It felt good to touch her leg after all the times when there had been itches and she hadn't been able to scratch because of the cast. Dr. Schertle promised that in a few days, after the leg had been exposed to good fresh air, her legs would match.

It was wonderful to walk out of the doctor's office without crutches. It was wonderful to take a real bath that night instead of a speedy shower with her cast wrapped in plastic. And it was wonderful to put shoes on both feet when she got dressed to go to school the next morning.

Cricket put on her sneakers. Then she reconsidered. Maybe she should wear her blue lace-up shoes. Or what about her red shoes with the buckles? She put a blue shoe on one foot and a red shoe on the other as she tried to make her decision.

"Cricket," Mr. Kaufman called up the stairs to his daughter.

Cricket walked to the door of her room and called down to him. "What do you want, Dad?" she asked.

"Let me drive you to school one last time today," he said. "I have an appointment that takes me right past your school building."

"Okay," Cricket agreed. It would be more dramatic to arrive at school in her new castless state than to walk there and have kids see her along the route.

Cricket gathered up her books and stuffed them into her backpack.

At the front of the school building Cricket's father leaned over and gave her a hug. "I may never drive you to school again," he said. "You're becoming such a big young lady."

"That's okay, Dad," she told him. "You'll have Monica to drive to school before long."

"Right," he said. "Have a great day!"

Cricket waved to her father and ran happily into the building. She wanted to show Mr. Flores that her heavy plaster cast was gone and that all she wore now was the light air brace.

"Look at me!" she called out to him as she entered the classroom.

Mr. Flores was in the back of the room, tacking up a poster on the wall.

He turned to face Cricket.

"Look," she said proudly. "I don't have a cast anymore." As she spoke, she looked down at her feet.

"Oh, no!" she groaned. "I can't believe it."

"What's wrong?" asked Mr. Flores. He came toward Cricket. "Is your ankle hurting you?"

"Look," said Cricket, blushing. "I came to school wearing two different shoes."

"Well. So you did." Mr. Flores laughed.

"It's so embarrassing," said Cricket. Whoever heard of wearing two different shoes to school?

"It's not so terrible," said Mr. Flores. "The important thing is that you don't need the cast anymore and that your break is all healed."

"But it looks stupid," Cricket protested. This was not the way she wanted to look at all.

Just then Zoe came into the classroom. Cricket had phoned her the night before, so Zoe already knew that her friend was no longer wearing a cast.

"Oh, Zoe. I did such a dumb thing," said Cricket, turning to her friend for comfort. A man like Mr. Flores couldn't know what it would feel like to be a girl and to be wearing shoes that didn't match. Zoe would understand.

Sure enough, when Zoe looked at Cricket's feet, she was properly sympathetic. "Keep your feet under your desk," she suggested. "That way hardly anyone will notice."

"But what about when I walk in the hall to go

to lunch or music?" Cricket shuddered. This day, which she had anticipated for so many weeks, was turning out to be awful.

Zoe stood looking at Cricket's feet. "What size are your shoes?" she asked.

"Four," said Cricket.

It was funny. The girls had been best friends for two years now, and it was one piece of information that hadn't been shared.

"Too bad," said Zoe. "If we had the same size, I could take one of them from you. I'll be back very fast," she promised, and rushed out of the room.

Cricket wondered what Zoe meant about taking one of her shoes. She sat down at her seat and tucked her feet underneath the desk. She had planned to be standing when her classmates entered the room. She had wanted them to notice the absence of her cast and to see the air brace. Now she just hoped no one would look down at her ankles and feet at all.

The students began walking into the room. "Hi, Cricket," Lucas called to her. "It was so warm last night that my father said it's almost time for crickets. He meant *real* crickets, of course."

"I'm a real Cricket," said Cricket. "A real person named Cricket, that is."

No one but Lucas Cott ever seemed so fascinated by her name. He was probably jealous and wished his name was as interesting as hers.

Just then Zoe and Sara Jane came rushing into the room together. "Look," Zoe called to Cricket. "It's great luck. We both wear size five."

Cricket looked down at Zoe's feet. She had a red sneaker on her right foot and a white one on her left. Then she saw that Sara Jane had a red sneaker on her left foot and a white one on her right.

"We're going to start a new style," Zoe promised her friend. "I bet by tomorrow all the girls in all the fifth grades will come to school wearing different shoes."

"It's a little weird," said Sara Jane. "But Zoe said that since the three of us are doing it at the same time, no one will laugh at us."

"Yes, they will," said Cricket happily. She was laughing herself. What a good friend Zoe was to think of such a thing. And it was great that Sara Jane was helping her out today too. She jumped up and hugged both girls. "We'll be like the Three Musketeers. In a couple of days we'll have to think of something else to make us different from everyone else."

"Me too?" asked Sara Jane.

"Sure," said Zoe. "We're all friends, aren't we?"

"All for one and one for all," exclaimed Cricket, quoting from *The Three Musketeers*. Her father had rented the video of that film for her during spring break.

In a couple of minutes everyone was seated and the school day was ready to begin. It turned out to be a great day, just as Cricket had hoped it would.

"Cricket Gets a Letter

The school year was drawing to a close. The students had finished their math workbooks and were doing review problems that Mr. Flores gave them on photocopied sheets. Outdoors the weather had turned warm enough that Cricket needed to wear only a light sweater when she left home in the morning to go to school.

One warm and sunny June day Mr. Flores suggested to the students that they take their lunches and walk to the nearby park for a picnic. Julio, who bought his lunch every day, had to rush to the lunchroom to buy a sandwich to take with him. Everyone had such a good time at this unexpected picnic that Julio didn't even complain that he'd had to forfeit the school hot lunch of spaghetti and meatballs, sliced cucumbers, and fruit cocktail.

There were a couple of half days when the students went to school just in the morning and had the afternoon off.

"I'm going with my mother to buy clothes for sleepaway camp," Lucas announced on the second of the half days. He made a face. "I'd rather stay in school than go shopping."

No one else agreed with him. Everyone liked this little taste of the vacation period that was soon to come.

"What are you going to do this afternoon?" Julio asked Mr. Flores.

"When you have a half day, teachers have afternoon meetings. We have to plan the curriculum for next year."

"Poor you, not having the afternoon off," said Cricket. She was going to spend the afternoon with Zoe and Sara Jane. She still couldn't go skating or bike riding, but the girls could always think of less active things to keep them busy. Today they were going to Zoe's house for lunch. Afterward they were going to play beauty parlor.

The plan was to borrow Zoe's sister Halley's nail polish and give one another manicures. They were going to try new ways of combing their hair too. Cricket had discovered that there were lots of activities that were more fun with three than with two.

Mr. Kaufman picked Cricket up at Zoe's house shortly after five o'clock. Cricket could have walked home, but her parents were still babying her a bit because of her ankle.

"Hop in, Sara Jane. I'll give you a ride too," offered Cricket's father.

"Do you notice anything different?" Cricket asked him.

He looked at her and smiled. "No. Should I?"

"My hair," Cricket hinted. "Can't you tell it's different?"

Mr. Kaufman looked at her. "It's still on your head," he observed. "And it's the same color that it was this morning."

"Oh, Daddy." Cricket giggled. "It's parted on the left side. This morning it was parted on the right."

"Oh," said Mr. Kaufman. "Of course. I don't

know why I didn't notice. You look beautiful." He turned to look at Sara Jane. "I'm not sure what you did to yourself," he admitted, "but you look beautiful too."

"I'm wearing my hair loose now. This morning I had it pinned back with barrettes," said Sara Jane. "But you didn't see me this morning. So you couldn't know that."

"Right." Then Mr. Kaufman asked Sara Jane for her address and drove off in that direction. It wasn't until Sara Jane had left the car that he turned to Cricket and made an announcement. "Your mother said there is a letter at home from the postal system."

"Postal system?" asked Cricket. It took her a moment to realize what that meant. She'd been so busy now that her ankle was healed that she hadn't been thinking about the contest lately.

"Do you think that means I won?" she asked eagerly.

"Your mother didn't open the envelope. So we won't find out until we're home," said Mr. Kaufman. "I suspect that they would notify the contestants either way. But whether you win or lose the contest, you're always a winner to me. To your *mother* and me," said Cricket's father, correcting himself.

Cricket could hardly sit still. "Can't you go any faster?" she asked her father. She wanted to get home and open the envelope at once.

"Not without breaking all the traffic regulations," said Mr. Kaufman as he stopped for a red light.

"I just can't wait to see what it says inside the envelope," said Cricket.

"Start counting," instructed Mr. Kaufman. "We'll be home before you reach a hundred."

"That's silly," said Cricket, but she had nothing better to do, so she began to count. "One . . . two . . . three . . ." Cricket reached eighty-four as the car pulled into the driveway of her home.

She unhooked her seat belt and opened the car door.

"Watch your step," shouted Mr. Kaufman as Cricket went running toward the house. "You don't want to fall and break your other ankle."

Cricket hardly heard her father's words. She pulled open the door to the house and ran inside. "Mom," she shouted. "Mom, I'm home. Where's the letter for me?"

Mrs. Kaufman came from the kitchen, holding a carrot in her hand. "Hi, sweetie," she said, kissing the top of her daughter's head.

Cricket forgot to ask her mother if she liked the way her hair looked parted on the left side. She didn't remember to show her the pink peony polish on her fingernails either.

"Where's the letter?" Cricket repeated.

"Just a minute," said her mother. "Your father and I want to tell you something before you read the letter."

"What?" asked Cricket, jumping from one foot to the other. How could she wait another minute to find out about the contest?

"The fact is," said Mr. Kaufman, coming into the room and putting his arm around Cricket, "your mother and I know how disappointed you were that you couldn't go to Washington this spring. And we've been talking about how we can arrange for you to make a trip there."

"Really?" asked Cricket in surprise.

"Yes. A trip to Washington would be an educational experience, and it doesn't seem fair to make you wait until Monica is old enough to appreciate the experience too."

Cricket nodded her head. That was exactly what she had told her parents back in April when she had broken her ankle.

"So regardless of whether or not you win the

contest," her father continued, "we want you to know you can look forward to a trip to Washington."

"When?" asked Cricket. "When can I go?"

"We thought when school was over, in two weeks. Grandma Diana said that she'd come and stay here with Monica. And you and I could go to Washington for two or three days," said her mother.

"What about you?" Cricket asked her father.

"It won't be a good time for me to take off from work," said Mr. Kaufman. "But you and your mother could have a really good time together."

"Oh, that's wonderful," said Cricket. She threw her arms around her mother and then her father. Then she thought of something.

"Could we invite Sara Jane to go with us?" she asked.

"Sara Jane?" asked her mother, sounding surprised.

"She didn't go with Zoe either. And I think she really feels bad about it. If she had a couple of weeks to get used to the idea, I think she'd come with us. And I think she wouldn't get homesick."

"If her parents agree, it would be fine with me," said Mrs. Kaufman. She walked toward the piano, where she had placed the envelope addressed to Cricket. "I almost opened it for you," she admitted.

"How could you open it for me?" asked Cricket in amazement. "It's addressed to *me,* not you."

"That's true," said her mother, smiling. "But I've become just as excited as you about the contest," she admitted. "And I'd have called you at Zoe's house if there was good news."

"I'm glad you didn't open it," said Cricket. She took the envelope from her mother and eagerly ripped it open. As she tore the envelope, she suddenly realized that the joy of winning or the disappointment of losing was ahead of her. So she paused before pulling out the letter and reading it. Until she read what was written, it was possible that she had won.

> *Dear Cricket Kaufman,*
>
> *Children like yourself, ages eight to thirteen and from all fifty states, submitted one hundred and fifty thousand entries to the national stamp design contest. The contest truly proved that kids really care about the environment. The entries were so wonderful that the judges would have liked to have one hundred and fifty thousand winners. Unfortunately, only four designs could be chosen.*

We regret to tell you that your entry was not one of the winners. However, you can be proud of the work you did. Next March, when the new stamps are printed and circulated, you can look at them with pride and know that you took part in the first national student competition.

Thank you for your submission. We hope you will continue in your concern for the environment.

Cricket stared at the words in the letter. Somehow she hadn't really expected to win such a big contest. She hadn't won a five-hundred-dollar savings bond. And next spring no one would be pasting her stamp on any letters. But it didn't really matter now. Entering the contest had been fun in itself. Now she could look forward to her trip to Washington.

She'd get Zoe to help her convince Sara Jane what a good time she would have. It was important for Sara Jane to know she wasn't a baby and could take an overnight trip. They could have their pictures taken with the cardboard statues of the president and the first lady. Maybe they would even meet the president in person. It was unlikely, but who knew? Anything was possible. This morning she had never dreamed that she'd be going to Washington in two weeks.

Mrs. Kaufman picked up the carrot she had placed on the piano.

"Better wash your hands," she told Cricket. "Supper is almost ready."

Cricket nodded her head and smiled. Even though she loved school, she knew she was going to be counting the days till the end of fifth grade. She had so much to look forward to.